A PLANESWALKER'S GUIDE is your best resource for insider information on the Multiverse's most exotic planar destinations. Our expert planar travelers share their advice and experiences in an organized and convenient way, so you can spend your trip enjoying the sights and sounds of your destination rather than performing divinations and rummaging through ancient tomes. Be sure to seek out other volumes in the PLANESWALKER'S GUIDE series.

A Planeswalker's Guide to Alara

Doug Beyer
Jenna Helland

A Planeswalker's Guide to Alara

Authors
Doug Beyer & Jenna Helland

Cover Artist
Raymond Swanland

Concept Artists
Chippy
Wayne Reynolds
Richard Whitters
Zoltan Boros & Gabor Szikszai
Dan Scott
Cyril Van Der Haegen

Editor
Philip Athans

Graphic Designers
Emi Tanji, Trish Yochum, with
Keven Smith

Art Directors
Matt Adelsperger, Karin Powell

World Design
Brady Dommermuth
with contributions from
Doug Beyer
Jennifer Clarke Wilkes
Jenna Helland
Cormac Russell

MAGIC Creative Director
Brady Dommermuth

MAGIC Senior Art Director
Jeremy Jarvis

Proofreader
Andrea Sehestedt

Published by Wizards of the Coast, Inc. MAGIC: THE GATHERING, WIZARDS OF THE COAST, and their respective logos are trademarks of Wizards of the Coast, Inc., in the U.S.A. and other countries.

Printed in the U.S.A.

First Printing: September 2008

Cataloging in Publication data is available from the Library of Congress.

9 8 7 6 5 4 3 2 1

ISBN: 978-0-7869-5124-6
620-21995740-001-EN

U.S., CANADA,
ASIA, PACIFIC, & LATIN AMERICA
Wizards of the Coast, Inc.
P.O. Box 707
Renton, WA 98057-0707
+1-800-324-6496

EUROPEAN HEADQUARTERS
Hasbro UK Ltd
Caswell Way
Newport, Gwent NP9 0YH
GREAT BRITAIN
Save this address for your records.

Visit our web site at www.wizards.com

MAGIC
The Gathering ®

Lorwyn
Cory J. Herndon &
Scott McGough

Eventide
Scott McGough &
Cory J. Herndon

Morningtide
Cory J. Herndon &
Scott McGough

Time Spiral
Scott McGough

Shadowmoor
Edited by
Susan Morris &
Philip Athans

Planar Chaos
Scott McGough &
Timothy Sanders

Future Sight
Scott McGough &
John Delaney

CONTENTS

ZOLTAN BOROS & GABORSZIKSZAI, VOLKAN BAGA

A
PLANESWALKER'S
GUIDE TO
ALARA

HOW TO USE THIS GUIDE

Welcome to *A Planeswalker's Guide to Alara*, your tour guide through the plane of Alara, its history and origins, its resident planeswalkers, and of course its five remarkable shards. This chapter gives an overview of Alara, covering the essential destinations within its sub-planes. The next five chapters cover each of those sub-planes in detail, with crucial information about the environment, terrain, creatures, cultures, and magic of each shard. The last chapter includes in-depth profiles of the known planeswalkers currently in residence on the shards of Alara.

Each chapter, written by our staff of expert researchers who have traveled to Alara, is fully illustrated with thumbnail sketches and artists' renderings of the spectacles and attractions you'll experience during your travels there.

JAIME JONES, DAN SCOTT

THE ORIGIN OF ALARA'S SHARDS

The plane of Alara was once a single, immense plane, rich in mana and natural resources. Unfortunately, we can only imagine that world now; Alara as such is no more. Many centuries ago, Alara was stripped of its mana in a cataclysmic planar event, perhaps brought on by the actions of a long-lost planeswalker. The drain on Alara's mana shattered something deep in its metaphysical structure, causing it to undergo a radical planar refraction. The plane broke into shards along mana lines, diffusing into its component parts like light refracted in a prism—and shattering Alara's civilizations and ecologies along with it. Whatever agent caused this destruction abandoned what remained of the plane, its spell presumably finished.

THE SHARDS' IDENTITIES

The shards that resulted from Alara's refraction drifted away from each other in the Blind Eternities. They were planes unto themselves, but not complete—each was cut off from two different colors of mana. The plane that became known as Bant, for example, lost its connection with black and red mana. The plane of Jund was severed from its blue and white, and so on.

As the shards' mana supplies slowly replenished themselves again, this mana imbalance dramatically altered life on each world. Environments warped to match the changed mana landscape, and life changed with it. Many species fell to extinction, while new forms of life adapted and prospered. On Esper, without wild green or red magic, nature fell by the wayside, while all-controlling wizards rose to ascendancy. Grixis, lacking the life magic of green and white, became a realm of undeath and necromancy. In this way, each shard evolved to become its own unique world.

The Shards of Alara Today

Today, Alara's once-great empires lie forgotten under layers of Alara's contemporary, mana-adapted civilizations. Each shard has developed its own distinctive identity in the centuries apart from its mother plane, making Alara an amazing opportunity to witness extreme contrasts with relatively little travel.

Bant at a Glance

Ruled by the hierarchy of angels that fill its crystal blue heavens, Bant is a natural and cultural utopia. Castle spires rise majestically over golden fields. The sun reflects in the polished armor of rows of knights. A rigid caste system determines the role of every member of society, yet corruption is nowhere to be found. Bant is a plane where true community has found a home.

ESPER AT A GLANCE

Esper is a world where powerful magic has trumped nature. Human and vedalken mages control almost every aspect of life here, from the tides and winds to the shortcomings of the flesh. An agency called the Ethersworn have made it their mission to infuse a magical alloy called etherium into every living creature on the plane, following the doctrine of the plane's enigmatic sphinxes.

GRIXIS AT A GLANCE

Grixis is no place for novice travelers. Swarms of undead, rampant death magic, and demonic influence make Grixis an abominable destination best avoided by most. However, Grixis is home to some of the shrewdest forms of necromancy practiced anywhere in the Multiverse; if you seek knowledge of the undead or necromantic practices, it can be a worthy plane to study.

JUND AT A GLANCE

Jund is a plane-spanning web of predation crowned by dragons. Nature is in its rawest, most treacherous state here, devouring all not prepared for its dangers. Whether you face Jund's human warrior tribes, its packs of viashino hunters, its mighty dragons, or simply its carnivorous flora, your survival skills will be tested to their fullest. It's saying something that feisty goblins, who cling desperately to the bottom of Jund's food chain, are the safest foes you'll face.

NAYA AT A GLANCE

As a tropical jungle-plane peopled with perfect specimens of the human, elvish, and leonin races, Naya seems like a paradise. But don't let its exuberant cultures fool you; Naya tremors with peril. Behemoths taller than buildings lumber through Naya's rainforests, crushing acres of vegetation—or civilization—casually underfoot. Yet somehow, Naya's sentient races revere these gargantuans, relegating them to the pinnacle of their religious beliefs and ascribing to them a sacred ineffability. Travelers will surely experience culture shock of the tallest order among Naya's vine-dense glades.

YOUR TRAVELING IDENTITY

Many planeswalkers favor discretion when traveling. If you choose to mask your identity as a planeswalker while traveling to Alara, you may not even need to prepare illusion magic. Human planeswalkers have it easiest, as humans are native to every shard of Alara—but be aware of the appearance of the humans of the shard you're visiting. On Bant, humans are regal and severe with pale or olive-colored skin.

Esper's humans are tall, slight, and infused with etherium enhancements. The humans of Grixis are often ashen and bloated with disease. On Jund they are sinewy and fierce, and some even have slightly reptilian features. Naya's humans are singularly beautiful, idealizations of the human form. Make sure to study the costuming of the planes' humans in their respective chapters.

If you are not human or do not wish to appear human, Alara's shards are home to many more humanoid races with whom to blend in or impersonate. On Bant are several species of avens, rhino creatures known as rhoxes, and angels. Vedalken make up a large majority of Esper's sentient population, and there are also magically constructed creatures called homunculi. Aside from the undead, Grixis supports ogres, vulturelike avens called kathari, and demons. Jund has a burly, crocodilian race of viashino, a rodent-like species of goblin, and elementals of all descriptions. On Naya you can find an elegant race of jungle elves and several varieties of fierce Nacatl leonin.

Missing Mana

Since Alara refracted into shard-planes, each shard has lacked two colors of mana, making certain types of magic impossible there. The natural phenomena normally associated with the missing colors still occur, just not the magic that manipulates them. For example, Bant, lacking black and red mana, has never seen pyromancy or necromancy. But its denizens still experiences mundane fire, and of course, mortality. Magic of growth, protection, and knowledge flourish there.

Spellcasting on the Shards

As a traveler to the shards, you should understand the consequences of this missing mana to your own spellcasting. While on Bant, your mana bonds to otherplanar mountains and swamps should function normally, but you'll be unable to establish new mana bonds to sources of red and black mana while there. To keep your identity as a planeswalker secret, it is imperative that you limit the use of magic that would be impossible on the shard. Our researchers recommend you emulate the magic of the plane's native mages so as not to arouse suspicion.

RAYMOND SWANLAND, VANCE KOVACS, MATT STEWART

ALARA'S OBELISKS

When Alara was one plane, mages channeled and filtered its rich sources of mana with enormous artifacts called obelisks. The obelisks tamed Alara's wild mana into easily manageable sources for rituals, summonings, and other spellcraft. With such powerful and reliable mana, Alara, in its early days, was one of the Multiverse's most accommodating environments for spellcasters.

When Alara fractured into shards, the obelisks remained on each plane, but with the mana drained and cultures reeling from the changes, the artifacts soon fell into disuse and disrepair. Over time, as each shard developed its own identity, the obelisks' mana-channeling purpose was forgotten. Some were reclaimed by the wilderness. Others now serve as temples or sacrificial altars for contemporary systems of belief.

Our research indicates, however, that the obelisks now hum with mana once again. Though the mages who knew the techniques to maintain them are long dead, and the mana flowing on each shard is incomplete, the obelisks have recovered their ability to channel what mana remains.

Today the obelisks are among the prime attractions of Alara, and one of its few features in common across all the shards. Despite their differences in appearance, they are a link to Alara's common past, a window onto a time before the world shattered, and collectively, a symbol of the distinctive identities Alara's progeny have evolved since.

DAVID PALUMBO, FRANCIS TSAI, NILS HAMM, BRANDON KITKOUSKI, STEVE PRESCOTT, ANTHONY FRANCISCO

COULD ALARA RECONVERGE?

When Alara's mana was drained and the plane became fragmented, the five shards were likely propelled apart into the chaotic void of the Blind Eternities. Yet today they are relatively close to one another: a puzzle. The circumstances suggest one of two possibilities. On the one hand, the shards may never have strayed far from one another since the initial rupturing. But our experts believe that Alara was the site of an extremely powerful outburst long ago, as indicated by the ætheric rippling observed around the planes today. The evidence isn't unassailable, but it's thought that the shards, when they first separated, should have drifted farther apart.

The other view is that the shards may have, at some point in time, stopped moving away from each other, and have begun reconverging again. Why this might be so is not known. The so-called "streaks" in the æther around Alara's cluster of shards may be consistent with the trails of shard-planes headed toward one another. However, the trajectories don't match expectations. The "streaks" may represent some other phenomenon.

Alara has been rediscovered by planeswalkers only relatively recently; no long-term research has been conducted. There is not enough evidence to warrant adoption of either hypothesis at this time, nor is it known what might happen if the shards do converge. Some have taken the reconvergence hypothesis as a reason to visit Alara now, and this is as good a reason as any.

BANT

The Plane of Bant

Built on a rocky cliff, a pristine white castle overlooks a cerulean sea. Fortified walls encircle a courtyard filled with fig trees and neatly tended gardens. At each corner is a round tower, their bronze roofs gleaming in the sunlight. Suspended between the towers is an elevated keep that houses a noble family and a regiment of knights who would fight to the death to defend the honor of their station. An angel flies high above the castle and continues east over the rolling green plains and domed roofs of the rhox monasteries that dot the countryside. She is one of many angels that watch over the orderly, rule-bound communities that inhabit the temperate plane below her.

This is Bant, a place of fortified towns, ritualized warfare, and the endless quest for honor. The nations of Jhess and Valeron control the coastal regions while the inland savannahs are divided between the three nations of Akrasa, Topa, and Eos. Despite periodic wars between the nations, they all share the same code: knightly orders defend the natural law, heroic men and women wear enchanted medallions known as sigils, and everyone trains in weaponry and martial arts from a very early age.

MATT STEWART, GREG STAPLES

The Races of Bant

Rhoxes, avens, humans, and leotau are the most common races in Bant. While rhoxes, avens, and humans can be found throughout the plane, leotau prefer the inland savannahs and have a notorious dislike of the ocean and coastal areas.

Rhoxes

Warrior-monks and ascetics, the rhoxes have a solitary nature combined with an innate dedication to spiritual contemplation. They have a reputation for physical prowess and an impatience for those who disagree with them. Those rhoxes that don't turn to spiritual retreat usually become muscle in groups of Unbeholden, the lawless caste that have turned against the rules of Bant society.

Avens

A proud race of winged warriors and mages, the avens' homeland is a swath of rocky highland jutting out of the savannah on land claimed by the nation of Akrasa. Though they follow the caste system, many avens avoid entanglement in human affairs. Humans consider avens to be somehow akin to angels— if for no other reason than their appearance. Avens are a bit puzzled by this elevated status because they don't worship the angelic guardians of the plane in the same way the humans do.

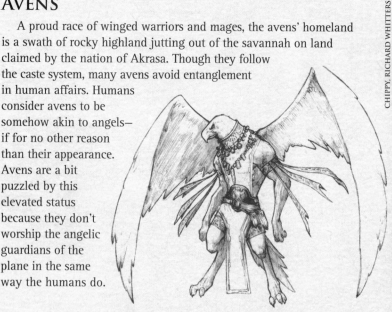

CHIPPY, RICHARD WHITTERS

HUMANS

Segmented into a caste-based society, humans follow a rigid code of honor and discipline. From an early age, children are taught a weapons-based martial art known as *Halcou*, a name derived from an alabaster bird with legendary grace and speed. While most humans strive for a life of honor and order, perfection is as impossible here as anywhere else. Some choose not to follow the rules of society and prefer to live as bandits and thieves.

WAYNE REYNOLDS

LEOTAU

Knights of the Inner Three nations ride semi-intelligent feline mounts. Neither Jhess nor Valeron use the leotau, for they are creatures of the vast savannah. There are three distinct leotau subspecies: the white-coated orisil favored by the Blessed caste; the golden, fleet-footed mherva; and the large, calico/dappled grohm.

ANGELS

Though they're mortal, angels are not born the way humans are. Rather, they are formed as a result of an ages-old enchantment that affects all of Bant. Whenever a hero dies, his or her soul transmutes into an angelic state. A hero is any "born" mortal who conformed to Bant's high ideals of honor and valor. Once a soul has transcended, an angel's body is comprised of "meta-sigils," the physical manifestations of world-magic drawn from the essence of the land and sky.

Angels gather at the Cathedral of Bliss, a vast temple of glowing marble and light that floats in the sky above Bant—higher than even the aven can fly. Ruled by the angel Asha, they can observe all of Bant and tend to their responsibilities. Angels embody the largest ideals, such as justice and truth. But they also embody the smallest concepts of beauty and perfection that many of the grounded races take for granted: the path of a crystalline stream flowing through a meadow, or the windswept silhouette of a tree against the dusky sky.

ANGELIC RANKS

Angels protect and cherish life, but they're not supposed to interfere in the political maneuverings or prosaic manipulations of lesser mortals. They may champion a cause, guide, and teach, but they do not lead, command, or order.

The angels have organized themselves into four discrete ranks:

Asura

There are seven angels Asura who form the Court of Orderly Contemplation.

Amesha

The angels Amesha are the embodiments of the grandest ideals that shape the lives of Bant mortals and inspire its knightly orders: honor, justice, truth, and courtly love.

Mahra

The angels Mahra are the angelic bureaucracy responsible for managing the implementation of the plans and orders of the Asura and Amesha.

Celebrant

The lowest rank of angel, Celebrants are responsible for protecting the day-to-day lives and ideals of lower castes. The activities of the Celebrants can range from selfless acts, such as giving food to the poor, or acts of whimsy, such as accompanying Adulai the Fool, the dancing monk, in his travels across the savannah of Topa.

THE CASTE SYSTEM

Every nation in Bant recognizes the same castes. Caste is set at birth, and breaking caste roles is rare. Pretending to a higher caste is punishable by imprisonment, while taking on a lower caste role results in a loss of caste to that level. Gaining sigils, the magic-infused medallions that symbolize allegiance and honor, is the only way to a higher level.

Blessed

Members of this noble caste interact with angels, lead nations, and live in accordance with the highest ideals. Many believe that when Blessed children are born, they will become angels as long as they don't fall into decadence or lawlessness. Members of the lesser castes must work harder and accomplish more noble deeds if they want their souls to transcend to the higher state.

Sighted

A spiritualist and clerical caste that includes many ascetic rhox monks. The Sighted need not bow before anyone, though they must obey the orders of the Blessed. Strangely, the angels and the Sighted have no special relationship. While the angels are seen as spiritual beings of great importance, the Sighted feel they have their own insights into such things, and don't rely on the authority of the angels in the same way as the other castes.

Sigiled

Through noble or courageous deeds, people can earn favor from a patron. Patrons can be high-ranking nobles, knights, or angels who may bestow sigils, magic-infused medallions that empower the wearer and increase their rank in society. Members of this caste are ranked by the number of sigils they bear.

Mortar

Most sentient creatures are Mortar. Mortars must follow the orders of the Sigiled, the Sighted, and the Blessed, though in the enlightened nations of Bant, such orders "are not given lightly. The Mortar are considered to be the keepers of common sense, as a counterpoint to the spiritual abstraction of the Sighted and the strictly coded existence of the Sigiled.

Unbeholden

This caste consists of bandits and thieves—those who, without Letters of Marque, forcibly take personal possessions from others. The Unbeholden are often victims of circumstance or rebels who reject the caste system, but there are few truly vicious men and women among their ranks. Many families have one member who is part of the Unbeholden. Often their exploits are chronicled in fables meant to illustrate the importance of virtue and hard work, and the consequences of the lack of discipline that can lead to life as an Unbeholden.

Lisha of the Azure

    A tall, striking woman with dark blue eyes, Lisha's lips are always painted a brilliant azure blue. Lisha rejected her formal role as a princess of Jhess and became a privateer. Despite her royal family's disapproval, she sails the waters on her frigate, *Sunspray*, looting merchant ships along the coast of Jhess and Valeron.

    Lisha is known for taking a small share of the booty for herself, giving a larger portion to her crew, and distributing the rest to the poor. It isn't unusual for *Sunspray* to attack a Jhessian port, take over its warehouses, and hand out the contents to the local Mortars and Unbeholden. So far, Lisha has always escaped to her ship before the Jhessian cavalry could capture her.

SIGILS

Sigils are magic-infused marks of support and allegiance in Bant. Royal houses, nobles, knightly orders, towns, monasteries, angels, and even a few remarkable individuals are able to grant sigils to signify their support for someone. A few sigils can be bought, but most must be earned in combat or through noble deeds. All sigils empower their wearer. A sigil might increase a person's strength, or heal wounds, or boost endurance. There are rumors of dark sigils that existed before the angels scoured evil from the land.

Smile of Jhess

This sigil is available only to members of the royal family of Jhess, though rumor has it that Lisha has bestowed the sigil upon a few paragons that have earned her favor through acts of compassion or charity to the poor.

Serul Cove

Serul Cove is a coastal city whose sigil is granted to their sea captains. It grants the bearer free passage into the cove and the protection of their modest navy while in their waters.

Truth

Truth is earned by a decade of dedication to the so-called Ideal of Greatest Weight, and whoever bears the sigil becomes physically incapable of lying.

KNIGHTLY ORDERS

The major knightly orders are active in all the nations of Bant and provide a culturally unifying force. In general, members of an order will resist fighting one another, even when their kingdoms are at war.

The Skyward Eye

The order of the Skyward Eye is an embodiment of the ideal of righteousness. Striving for perfection in being good, living correctly as an example to others, and guiding others in their lives is the core duty of the order. The Skyward Eye crusades against groups and places that choose to not live correctly. Jhess in particular draws ire for its denizens' embrace of what members of the order see as hedonistic pursuits.

The Knights of the Reliquary

The Knights of the Reliquary are an itinerant order that have representatives throughout Bant. They spend their time searching the land for remnants of ancient times, though they don't know exactly what they're seeking, and they don't know exactly what they've found. But in their great warehouses are relics that point to an ancient civilization—a civilization that seemed to practice abhorrent, evil rites. The Knights of the Reliquary investigate any rumors of magical power and any discovery of new ruins.

The Wayfarers' Friends

The Wayfarers' Friends patrol the roads of Bant, keeping them safe from bandits and monsters. They maintain way stations in uninhabited areas and are the favored knightly order for Mortars who venture out to see the world.

MONKS

Human monasteries are both militaristic and spiritual, and monks divide their time between meditation and martial pursuits. Each monastery has a liturgy based on the martial art, *Halcou*, and monks practice this highly stylized combat system using a variety of single-handed weapons. Typically, monks commit to vows and prohibitions, such as a vow of poverty or a vow against deceit. Some of these vows become quite extreme, such as a sect that takes a vow of motion. They walk until they collapse in exhaustion only to get up and begin their endless journey again.

Many rhox monks are ascetics, seeking religious inspiration through meditation and a solitary life. If a religious dispute between a human monk and a rhox ascetic can't be resolved through debate, it may become a physical challenge. On an open field, each challenger demonstrates their spiritual fitness through elaborate displays of *Halcou*. While there is no "winner" of such displays of athleticism, the unspoken agreement is that the challenger with the most grace and skill has the deepest philosophical understanding of the issue in question.

THE GREAT STELES

Huge stone obelisks called steles dot the lands of Bant, focusing and channeling the energy of the land itself. Major forts are built around steles, and the magic from the obelisks seeps into the architecture and instills it with the strength of the surrounding countryside.

Steles are inscribed with detailed pictograms that illustrate a cycle of myths, and the art of carving the steles is a common rhox profession. Since very few humans have the strength to work the dense rock, rhoxes view themselves as the keepers of the myths and the only race to truly understand the symbolic meanings of the stories. One of the most famous steles sits on a peninsula of blue-tinged rock that juts into the rough ocean north of the port of Serul Cove. Known as the Cormorant Stele, it's engraved with massive seabirds engaged in battle with a sea monster. Rhox monks who make pilgrimages to the great stele swear that they return home with increased vitality and prowess in battle.

THE NATIONS OF BANT

Jhess and Valeron are coastal nations, and some traditionalists claim their seafaring cultures are too lax, particularly when it comes to caste. By contrast, the more conservative nations of Eos, Akrasa, and Topa strictly adhere to the rules of warfare and honor.

JHESS

The island nation of Jhess lies along the eastern coast of Bant. Jhessians are famous navigators and have the finest navy in Bant. They are currently at war with Valeron, raiding its coastal villages with their swift naval fleets. Jhess's sleek ships and highly skilled marines dominate the sea and beaches, but Valeron's hearty cavalry rule the inland battlefields.

Jhess is more freewheeling than the other nations of Bant, and many Jhessians have a flamboyant streak that is attributed to their coastal living. A far greater portion of the population is likely to either be Sigiled or Sighted than in other nations, and Jhess has the largest number of Unbeholden. Jhessians' upward and downward mobility among the castes is considered shockingly radical by the more traditional mores of the Inner Three.

VALERON

Valeron stretches along the southern coast of Bant, a land of vast rolling plains dotted with copses of trees. Valeronians are renowned for their beauty, and though the elves are gone from Bant, folklore says Valeronians have some elvish blood. Valeron is famed for the quality of its horses and the expertise of its cavalry. While Valeron cannot challenge Jhess on the sea, their cavalry is so swift that they can spot raiding forces approaching their villages and shift their cavalry rapidly to meet nearly any threat.

The Sun-Dappled Court

The Sun-Dappled Court is a topiary garden planted with thuja trees of immense size that are shaped to resemble the great steles scattered throughout the kingdoms. Each of the Twelve Trees represents a particular noble bloodline, but all of the families of the court are considered to be one tribe. The families of the Sun-Dappled Court rule Valeron justly, though they have a defensive streak that can lead to diplomatic issues with other nations.

THE INNER THREE

The nations of Bant's central savannah, Akrasa, Topa, and Eos, are called the Inner Three. In normal times their relations are good, marked by commerce and cultural exchange, but since Jhess and Valeron went to war, the Inner Three have become embroiled in conflict as well. Compared to the more chaotic style of conflict practiced by the coastal nations, war among the Inner Three is a thing of forms and rituals, carefully timed marches of vast infantry units, and long speeches before battles.

Eos

Eos is nominally Valeron's ally, due more to their own disputes with Topa than any particular affinity for the Valeronians. The rulers of Eos possess ancient documents that they feel give them claim to several key watering holes in Topa, a claim that Topa steadfastly denies. Eos is the home of the Olive Branch, a knightly order that seeks to broker peace and smooth the relations between all the nations of Bant. However, all attempts by the knights of the Olive Branch to mediate the dispute between Topa and Eos have failed.

CHRIS RAHN, TODD LOCKWOOD

Akrasa

Akrasa, sometimes called "The Sea of Grass," is a land of fertile plains all put to agriculture. Several knightly orders are based in Akrasa, and its own armies are quite large. Akrasa has the largest number of ancient towers and castles of any kingdom and the largest Blessed caste in Bant. While every other caste is well represented and respected, in Akrasa, the Blessed rule with the support of the military. When a Blessed speaks in Akrasa, the ground itself is said to listen.

Akrasa does not have any large bodies of mounted troops. Their knights ride leotau and are mostly Mortars who believe their martial experience gives them a higher status than other Mortars. Outside of Akrasa this is seen as utter pretension and many a brawl has started when a non-Akrasan refused to treat an Akrasan regimentarian with the respect that they believe they're due.

Topa

The open savannah of Topa is spotted with towns that surround the precious watering holes and great cloister-forts built near important religious locations. Most wild leotau live in Topa, and its knight-paragons are famed for their skill with these feline mounts. Topa's wild leotau often attack Valeron's horse herds so relations are never better than strained cordiality. At the moment they are in outright war as Topa has allied itself with Jhess. Topa is famous for its caravans, huge trains that carry goods, travelers, and entertainers from watering hole to watering hole.

Topans are master merchants, and compared to other nations they have a particularly large Mortar population, filled with scribes and accountants, merchants and traders. The small Blessed caste that rules Topa looks to both successful Mortars and visionary Sighted for guidance, and both castes have high level representatives on government advisory councils.

Rafiq of the Many

Rafiq is the Grand Champion of Sigils, Knight-Captain of the Reliquary. The highest-ranked Sigiled in all of Bant, he has attained so many sigils that he is known as Rafiq of the Many. A noble and pure warrior, he is a paladin of the highest calling. While holding true to Bantian ideals, Rafiq is friendly and open, an inspiration rather than a judge, having never forgotten his own lowly birth as a Mortar, the son of a baker.

Rafiq participates in most of the major battles fought in Bant, though which side he champions depends on the delicate balance of all the interests of his sigils. It is not unusual for him to fight for one side one day, and the other the next, as the merits of each side in the conflict's claims require.

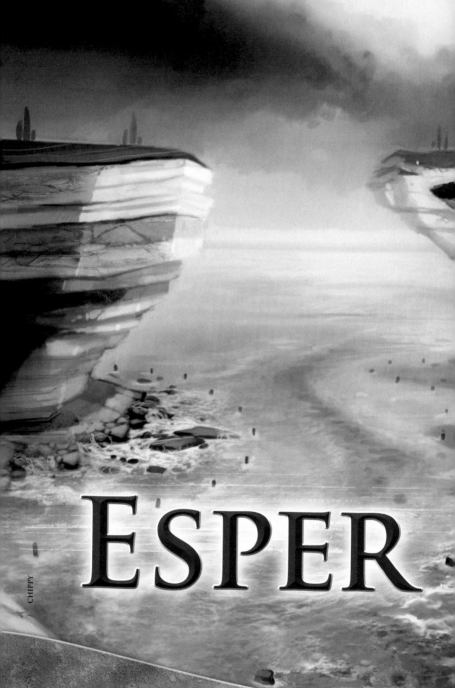

ESPER

CHIPPY

THE PLANE OF ESPER

Esper is a world where purpose and control have triumphed over savagery and chaos. Bereft of red and green mana, this plane's natural forces pale next to the supernatural power of its human and vedalken mages. Under the foresight of Esper's ruling sphinxes, the plane has transformed from wilderness to a tightly-controlled magocracy, with all forms of life perfected through the æther-infused metal known as etherium. Travelers to Esper should expect a spectacle of sophisticated beauty, where not only the plane but also its denizens have been meticulously designed according to a grand plan.

Terrain and Climate

A temperamental gray sky dominates the view wherever you travel in Esper. Towering clouds sliced along wizard-defined grid lines float over vast oceans, slate-colored islands, and deserts of glass. Without red or green mana, "wildlife" is not common here, but what the plane lacks in ferocity, it makes up for in the violence of wind and waves. Esper has strong winds and heavy downpours, the only elements of nature here not yet completely controlled by the sphinxes' magocracy.

ZOLTAN BOROS & GABOR SZIKSZAI, FRANZ VOHWINKEL

Oceans and Seas

Esper's oceans and seas typify all forms of marine geography, from the pitch-black Inkwell to the pale Dwindling Sea, from the placid Sea of Stars to the whirlpools of the Twin Maelstroms, from the vast Sea of Unknowing to the mysterious Kingdom of Fog. The vedalken set up tide control rudders to regulate the periodicity of the tides in most of Esper's waters, and tidemages help ships navigate through Esper's turbulent weather. Despite these advancements, what lurks beneath the sea here is still largely a mystery.

THE CLIFFS OF OT

These wind-carved cliffs hang improbably over a stretch of the Sea of Unknowing. Travelers are encouraged to listen to the whispers and wails in the sea spray; some Esperites believe the sounds are the voices of the dead. Vedalken, however, believe the cliffs are a place of mysticism, and that meditating on their heights will yield arcane insights.

THE GLASS DUNES

Esper's largest contiguous landscape is a large, glittering, white "sand" desert known as the Glass Dunes. Though normally calm, windstorms here can kick up the glass-dust and permanently blind those whose eyes aren't protected. Beneath the dunes, glacierlike masses of glass slowly accumulate through pressure and time.

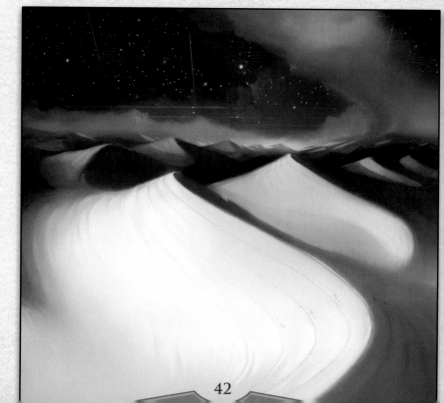

THE CESSPOOLS

Esper's cities and settlements are nothing if not clean. Waste material of all kinds is shipped to the Cesspools, deep pits where monstrous creatures swim through the ashen mulch and "process" the

refuse. The Cesspools have given rise to their own ghoulish ecosystem that Esper's civilized world does its best to avoid.

TIDEHOLLOW

A subterranean system of caverns, half-filled with darkened seawater, extends under Esper's largest islands. The seas' tides have worn the rock into a sort of honeycomb, a baffle for the crashing waves. The caverns continue for miles inland, providing good cover from the elements. Research indicates that Tidehollow may conceal evidence of long-dead cultures from Esper's ancient past, possibly related to the era of a unified Alara.

CLOUDHEATH AND THE ETERNAL STORM

Above a large, rocky expanse called Cloudheath, a storm with high winds and driving rain has been raging for over a century. A single tower stands in defiance of the storm, home to a single human hermit called Tiln. Tiln is an ancient, powerful, and irascible stormcaller. From time to time he will begrudgingly help guide a huge storm away from a major city, or rescue a vessel lost in the Kingdom of Fog.

ZOLTAN BOROS & GABOR SZIKSZAI, WARREN MAHY

ETHERIUM

Esperites believe all life is flawed and incomplete without an intrinsic connection to the æther, the essence of the universe. Through nonstop experimentation, they have devised complex magic that enables them to artificially supplement any living thing with etherium, a mysterious alloy infused with æther. Almost all living things on Esper have a small amount of etherium fused with their anatomy. The line between organic and artificial has not been totally eliminated here, but it has been blurred.

The methods of creating new etherium are only known to one sphinx, Crucius, whose whereabouts are unknown. Since his disappearance, Esper's existing etherium has been endlessly refined and attenuated into ever more delicate structures.

THE ETHERSWORN

The sanctioned order known as the Ethersworn serves a single purpose: to instill as many living things with etherium as they possibly can. As Esper's etherium supplies dwindle, their mission grows increasingly difficult, but members of the Ethersworn believe the metaphysical "fitness" of their entire world is at stake. In accordance with the teachings of the sphinx Crucius, they maintain that if enough of Esper's life is fused with etherium, the plane will transcend its mortal and physical limitations.

THE NOBLE WORK, THE IGNOBLE FLESH

The expression "the Noble Work" refers to the ongoing effort to instill every living thing on Esper with a small amount of etherium, thought to bring all beings closer to perfection. "The Ignoble Flesh" is the term for a splinter group who takes this philosophy to an extreme. Its adherents believe the flesh is fallible and impure and should be shed through the eventual replacement of the entire body with etherium. The very few who have achieved this goal are called æther-liches.

The Humans of Esper

On Esper, magic is synonymous with culture. The humans here are devoted, expert mages, and those with the most powerful magic rule the others. For this reason, Esper's history is peppered with occasional crude grabs at power, but each would-be tyrant has been swiftly put down. Subtlety goes much farther here than flashy magic or vulgar force.

Magical Specialization

Among the humans of Esper, specialization is key to establishing one's mastery. This is an incomplete list of such specialized mages:

Arcanist
A master of secret knowledge and lost lore.

Stormcaller
A wielder of weather magic.

Mechanist
An artificer with a talent for infusing complex creations with magic.

Clockworker
One who manipulates the forces of time.

Mentalist
A trafficker in thoughts, especially those others try to hide.

Tidemage
One who uses magic to influence the seas and tides.

In addition to these types one can also find the more standard voidmages, nullmages, pathmages, and so on. Some mages claim to know only one kind of magic, keeping their other skills to themselves.

RETINUES

Every mage of note has a personal retinue. The size and quality of a mage's retinue is an indicator of his or her clout and status. A powerful and influential mage might have a retinue of six or seven, including apprentices, telemins (see right), gargoyles, animal familiars, magically-created humanoids called homunculi, and even specimens of physical perfection just for show. Decorative tethers and leashes on members of one's retinue aren't uncommon, as a means of displaying who holds the reins—quite literally.

TELEMINS

A society founded on control needs individuals willing to be controlled. A voluntary "underclass" has emerged among Esper's humans—people willing to be the instruments of other mages' artistry. Telemins, sometimes called "mage dolls," allow themselves to be mentally commanded by a mage to perform some task, whether it's menial, skilled, or artistic. Credit for a telemin's skill or accomplishment never goes to the telemin himself but rather to the mage who "plays" him. Some telemins have become famous in the same way that a well-made instrument can become famous, like an exquisite violin.

NOTABLE HUMAN PLACES

Even outside of Vectis, Esper's largest human fortification, there are plenty of places to interact with humanity.

The House of Dialectics

The House of Dialectics is a sort of parliament chamber where the most influential human mages come to argue, convince, entreat, and bargain. Unlike vedalken society, human culture is not strictly hierarchical and is instead governed by influence, alliances, and debts of loyalty.

The Visitarium

This complex has a multitude of "visitation bays" in which humans can host other creatures for various transactions, whether they're for business, educational, or secretive purposes. Humans meet with vedalken visitors here, for example. There are large, central bays in which Esper's sphinxes land to discuss matters with the humans they deem worthy of their communication.

The Crypt of Knowledge

This sacred place is reserved for the clerics, who protect the arcane secrets and bodies of great archmages contained within it. Half tomb, half library, the Crypt of Knowledge is treated with the utmost respect. Speech is forbidden here, and documents and sepulchers are moved and manipulated telekinetically so as not to sully them by touch.

THE VEDALKEN OF ESPER

Vedalken are intelligent, progressive humanoids with skin tone that varies from a bluish white-gray to a dusky, deep blue. They have only the slightest indication of an outer ear, with no lobe or 'rim'—just a hole that leads to the eardrum. They have nostrils but only a slight nose bridge. They have only fine body hair that's uniformly clear and light.

Esper's vedalken are refined, sophisticated, and lawful, and have led Esper both in magical advancement and in the use of etherium. Whereas humans tend to have relatively minor and simple etherium enhancements, vedalken make more dramatic use of the alloy. It's not uncommon for vedalken necks or abdomens to be partially replaced with etherium, for example. In such instances, powerful enchantments stand in for traditional biological function.

MATT CAVOTTA, RICHARD WHITTERS & DAN SCOTT

Vedalken Psychology

In vedalken society, the pursuit of magic takes on an almost scientific purpose and methodology. The vedalken are driven to understand everything around them, and are thus in a constant, intense observational state. It can give other species the unnerving impression that they're being monitored and examined rather than talked to.

Artifact Devices and the Twenty-Three Winds

Orreries, astrolabes, observatories, meteorological charts, topographical models—all these things are like furniture to the vedalken. They are compulsive measurers and recorders of information of all kinds, but tend to focus on visual data. Vedalken have named all twenty-three winds of Esper, ascribing oracular import to their unique air currents.

THE FILIGREE TEXTS

The vedalken's search for enlightenment can be surprisingly spiritual. The vedalken study sacred grimoires called the Filigree Texts. These books contain all the information about Esper that the vedalken find significant, and weave that information into an obtuse kind of long-form poem. There are twenty-three tomes, one for each of their named winds. Several decades ago the vedalken augurs decided the tomes were sacred enough to be committed to etherium. Now each of the twenty-three codices consists of delicate, priceless etherium metal pages, with the text spelled out in the negative space between the filigree.

NOTABLE VEDALKEN PLACES

Vedalken architecture is among the most often recommended sights in the Multiverse, and the structures of Esper's vedalken exceed even the highest expectations. If you must choose two destinations, choose these, but each of Esper's vedalken-governed cities will inspire any devotee of art and architecture.

The Sanctum Arcanum

The Sanctum Arcanum is the glass-and-steel vedalken temple that houses the Filigree Texts. The atmosphere above it is enchanted so that it's never overcast; there's a kind of "hole in the clouds" that enables light to shine directly down into the structure. Many small academies have cropped up around the sanctum dedicated to studying the texts in specific contexts.

Palandius

The largest vedalken city, and considered a work of art by most vedalken, Palandius's dramatic architecture works with the natural terrain to create a dramatic, organic cityscape. It overlooks the Sea of Unknowing and is a major port for human-vedalken trade.

THE SPHINXES OF ESPER

Esper is home to a handful of great sphinxes, whose wisdom, magical prowess, and mastery over etherium makes them the rulers of the plane. Sphinxes prefer to remain a mystery to the humanoids, making their homes on distant, remote islands shrouded from view by magic. Their visits with humanoids are reasonably frequent, but sphinxes do not form lasting relationships. All sphinxes are vastly knowledgeable and insightful, but beyond that their characters vary widely, from cold and calculating to honorable and beneficent.

SHARUUM, THE HEGEMON

Sharuum is the beautiful, ageless female sphinx who serves as Esper's de facto "philosopher queen." Her word is taken as the deepest wisdom and her judgments, though rare, are incontrovertible. She cannot forge new etherium, but Sharuum has taught her allies how to thin the existing etherium, leading to ever more delicate filigree structures among Esper's beings.

CRUCIUS THE MAD

The sphinx Crucius was a seminal but
controversial figure in Esper history. Esperites now
revile the genius who brought etherium to the plane,
thinking him to have disappeared or died years ago.
But evidence suggests that he may have been a planeswalker,
and furthermore may have understood—and attempted
to correct—Esper's plight.

Decades ago, Crucius devised the magical alloy etherium and
began a grand project to infuse living things on Esper with it, which
he called the Noble Work. Records show that he proposed the Noble
Work as a means to overcome the frailties and limitations of the
mortal flesh, but Crucius may have in fact perceived Esper's
disconnection from two crucial elements, red and green mana.
Indeed, the æther inside etherium, once spread across enough of the
plane, may have been intended to enable a spell that would reunify
Esper with the other shards of Alara.

Reconvergence plan or no, the Noble Work became a kind of
dogma, and spun out of Crucius's control. Despite the sphinx's
attempts to warn them, Esperites began to replace more and more
of their flesh with etherium, eventually leading to the creation of
undead abominations called æther-liches. Crucius, as the source of
etherium, was blamed for the creatures, earning him the moniker
Crucius the Mad.

Ostracized and despondent, Crucius disappeared soon after.
Sharuum, Esper's sphinx hegemon, is the only one who may know
the truth of his true nature, his intentions, and his whereabouts.

WAYNE REYNOLDS, MICHAEL BRUINSMA

KEMUEL, THE HIDDEN ONE

One other sphinx bears noting. Kemuel, called the Hidden One, lives in a vast, complex maze deep within the Glass Dunes. He never leaves his inner chamber, partly because he is missing part of a wing and a rear leg—the result of a centuries-ago clash with a leviathan. The skies over the maze are kept turbulent by powerful magic so that none can bypass the labyrinth. Only the desperate dare to consult him, and many have died in the maze trying to reach him. The few that have reached him and have received his wisdom often find it baffling at first, but once understood it is tantamount to prophecy.

HOMUNCULI

A homunculus is a magically-created, living humanoid creature, created by the human alchemical masters of Esper. Homunculi are sentient and self-willed, but incapable of defying the demands of their creators. They are used for a myriad of purposes, but most often function as clerks, scribes, and couriers, and as decorative additions to mages' personal retinues.

Homunculi vaguely resemble small, "toy" versions of vedalken, which appears to make the vedalken uncomfortable around them. Whether humans intend a deeper symbolism in the homunculi's appearance—as homage to the wise and noble vedalken, or as a hint to some sinister origin of the creatures—is not known. Though the lives of homunculi aren't considered intrinsically valuable, humans keep them well protected, probably due to the labor and expense of their creation.

THE SEEKERS OF CARMOT

One sect of wizards, comprised of both humans and vedalken, has arisen recently on Esper. Their claim is that the etherium is running out, and that the way of life brought by the alloy will die out along with it. Their message has gained popularity in recent years as the etherium infusions of new generations have waned in size and complexity. The leaders of the sect claim that they have in their possession the partially destroyed, elaborately encoded *Codex Etherium* of the sphinx Crucius himself, and that they have decrypted the tome to the extent that they know they must find a red stone called carmot in order to unlock the secrets of etherium.

Carmot is indeed a component of etherium, though no trace of it has been found on Esper. The sphinx Crucius may somehow have consumed all of the material extant on the plane in his initial creation of etherium. Or it may be that Crucius was a planeswalker, able to obtain carmot from other shards of Alara.

OTHER CREATURES OF ESPER

Despite its sparse vegetation and lack of red and green mana, Esper is home to more than just humanoids. Among the creatures of Esper are gargoyles, drakes, birds, and several kinds of undead. Below Esper's seas lurk leviathans and krakens, some of them documented to predate even the oldest sphinxes.

GARGOYLES

The faithful servants of the most powerful mages in Vectis and Palandius, gargoyles serve as a living compromise between the world of flesh and the world of insensible objects. The first gargoyles on Esper were originally huge, elegantly carved statues perched on the tower abode of a former ruler of Palandius. They were brought to life with dramatic spells and an infusion of etherium to celebrate the ruler's ascendance to power. They proved so dedicated and practical that other, smaller gargoyles were animated for travel and guardianship.

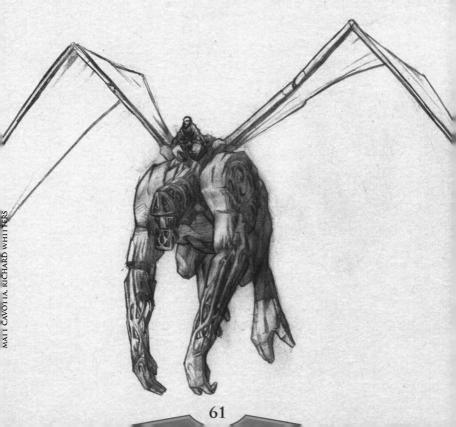

Ecology of the Cesspools

Esper's sludge-filled pits, the Cesspools, support their own ecosystems of strange creatures. Sluice serpents swim under the surface, eating whatever moves. Brinewraiths—vicious, incorporeal undead—are said to be the revenant spirits of those who died in water. Hauntcreeps, shadowy ghosts that drift around the Cesspools, make no sound other than a hissing white noise. And sludgestriders are monstrous insects that balance on the surface, feeding on passing refuse.

Tidehollow Scullers

The most fearsome sight in Esper may be the scullers, the undead boatmen of the tidecaves. When the weather on Esper's surface gets too inclement for extended journeys, some humans and vedalken will brave the Tidehollow and entrust their travel to them. Travelers to the plane should be aware that scullers use strange, nonverbal communication to negotiate their price, and only agree to unusual forms of payment. If you travel with a sculler, prepare to lose something of great and subtle value.

DRAKES

Drakes are dangerous predators on any plane, but the etherium-infused drakes of Esper should be treated with special caution. The sphinx Crucius—and those who now carry out his Noble Work, the Ethersworn—spent years perfecting their designs on drakes before infusing the first humanoid. As a result, hundreds or thousands of etherium-permeated drakes soar above Esper, many of which suffered strange behavioral changes as a result. One's usual instincts about drakes should not be trusted here.

STRIGES

Esper is home to a large, owl-like bird called a strix (collectively, striges). Striges resemble ashen-colored screech owls with deep black eyes. The screech of a strix can drain the thoughts and memories of those who hear it, which in turn nourishes the bird—a form of psychic vampirism.

GRIXIS

MARK TEDIN

THE PLANE OF GRIXIS

Grixis is a hellscape of decay and madness, a world founded on the axiom that power trumps death. Cut off from all sources of white or green mana, the remaining light and life of Grixis dwindle. The undead, mad necromancers, and demons all feed on the remaining scraps of life, exploiting the meek and enslaving the willful to realize their dark fantasies of power. Meanwhile the free-willed living scar their own hearts and minds for the sake of survival under the plane's cruel conditions. Travel to Grixis is recommended only for study or self-reflection—its value is not as spectacle, but as example.

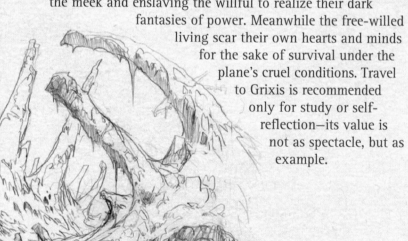

TERRAIN AND CLIMATE

Grixis's landscape does not look (or smell) healthy. Its skies are purple-gray, stormy, and ominous. Lightning cracks the earth and thunder tolls doom. Its hills are drifts of bones, its valleys are decaying flesh, and its seas are murky, polluted deathtraps. Its cities are lairs of undead hordes and necromancer barons, and every parcel of land between them is a battlefield for their constant power struggles.

THE DREGSCAPE

A disgusting panorama of diseased, decaying flesh, the Dregscape is a vast swamp where degeneration is slowed to a crawl. The carcasses of centuries-old beasts and people linger here, slowly becoming a thick ichor. The Dregscape is the main feeding ground for the kathari (vulture aven) and a wellspring of black mana and corpses for necromancy.

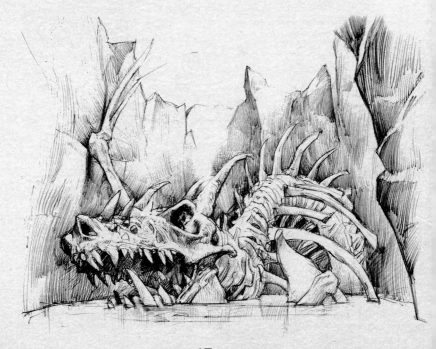

HISTORY

Before Grixis split off from Alara, it was the home of Vithia, a thriving human empire proud of its dynasty of wise and honorable monarchs. Vithian paladins were known for their crusades against the necromancers of old. But when the subplane broke away, not only was Vithia cut off from its access to white mana, the main source of its magic, but it also had to contend with the necromancers who rose to new heights of power. Vithian citizens became prey for the necromancers' armies, slaves to rogue demons, and victims of the treachery of corrupted Vithian rulers. When Sedris, the last of the Vithian kings, sold his kingdom and its citizenry to the first demon lords in exchange for the power of lichdom, the fractured plane became known as Grixis, after the Vithian word for "traitor." Today the lands of Vithia are in ruin and overrun with undead. The living that remain hide among the reminders of the past.

VITALS AND VIS

Most of the beings on Grixis are undead—or, like demons and other horrors, are neither living nor dead. Living beings, including humans, kathari, ogres, the occasional dragon, and some lowly vermin like insects, bats, and rats, are called "vitals" by the sentient undead. Vitals are the living, the vessels of life-essence so coveted by the undead of Grixis. This life-essence, the animating principle that makes a being alive, is called vis. Vis suffuses all tissues and bodily fluids of a living creature, but is not itself a physical material. Though it is also present in scant amounts in dead tissue, the vis present in living beings, suffusing living thoughts and desires, is far more vibrant and potent.

Despite its intangibility, vis is the most important resource on Grixis. On many planes, vis may be taken for granted, but Grixis is a world of death and decay. Black mana and its allies, blue and red mana, are plentiful and relatively easy to come by, but the magic of life is not. The mana of Grixis is entropic, self-destructive, without white and green mana to protect and strengthen it, it dissipates over time. As a result, Grixis, the plane of death, is itself dying. The only thing that extends its survival is vis.

Vis can be used to power necromancy and other magic that extends life—and unlife—against the overwhelming forces of decay that besiege the plane. Necromancers, horrors, and especially the undead crave vis to survive, and they reap it from corpses or vitals through any of several methods. Vis can be consumed directly from a living host via magical means, but is usually gathered through the blood or thoughts of the living. Spilled blood or a drained mind can be a powerful source of vis used for ritual magic.

THE DRONING ISLES

These crumbling towers of ashen crust are actually not islands at all, but enormous hives of insects called banewasps. Banewasps construct their hives in the middle of murky, shallow seas, which help protect their developing larvae from predators such as kathari and plague bats. The constant buzzing of these larva warehouses gives the Droning Isles their name.

THE BONE HEAPS

Once the kathari are done gnawing on a corpse, they fly the skeletons piece by piece to enormous hills of bones. There, rats and other vermin clean the rest of the meat from the bones and leave only clean, dry, clattering remains. The kathari can then use the pieces to construct animated skeletons, jewelry and armor, and bone golems. Bone heaps can be good sources of red and black mana, and are often scoured for valuables by the minions of necromancers and liches.

HERMITAGES

Living humans eke out an existence in small, brick hermitages. Some hermitages, wracked with the amnesia-magic of lethemancers and faced with the daily horrors of the plane, become nothing more than insane asylums. A precious few, such as the mountain fortress of Torchlight, are reasonably well-defended with sword and sorcery, but the renegades who maintain them are constantly under siege by flesh-hungry undead and tempted by the promises of demons.

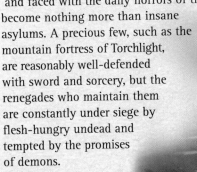

Necropolises

If there is any true civilization on Grixis, it's in the necropolises, cities of the undead. Most necropolises are ruled by liches or demon lords, but others are run by living necromancers. Rulers of necropolises, called barons, constantly war among one another, trying to expand their boundaries and hoards of resources. Some necropolises are built over enormous, labyrinthine systems of caverns that serve as dungeons for the living and storage for the dead.

Necropolis: Kederekt

Facetiously called "Seaside" by still-living Vithian humans, Kederekt is a series of large manor houses that border a sea of greasy, acidic water. The manor houses have sunken into the silt so they're tilted at odd angles. The residents are all undead, and Kederekt naturally divides them into those who live above and below the water line.

Necropolis: Unx

Unx was once a grand stadium, but its floor has become a huge sinkhole that leads far down to the magma below. Blackened, skeletal creatures skitter around the stone stands as though waiting for something to arise from the chasm.

Necropolis: Sedraxis

Sedraxis, the largest necropolis on Grixis, is the ruins of the Vithian capital. Filled with gothic arches and cobblestone streets, the once-great city is now a deadly maze of crumbling walls, half-collapsed spires, and roofless shells of buildings. The lich king Sedris "rules" this place, though he is usually content to let chaos reign within its walls.

Necromancers

Death is a powerful force, and necromancers harness it to fuel their magic. Death only occurs to the living, however, so most necromancers are, ironically, constantly in need of sources of life in order to work their spells. Where there is life there is vis, and vis powers Grixis. Therefore most necromancers use their powers to create minions, and use those minions to search for more sources of life.

Almost all necromancers are capable of animating dead tissue to do their bidding. But mages might practice more variants of necromancy on Grixis than on any other plane. Fleshcrafters—artists and artisans in the medium of death—create bizarre implements from flesh and bone. Lethemancers steal vis through the thoughts and memories of living beings, leaving amnesiacs and lunatics in their wake. Ghostslavers specialize in trapping and binding the restless spirits that haunt Grixis, while gale mages control the death gales, the entropic winds that scour the plane.

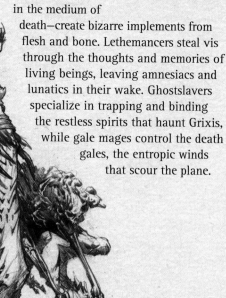

WAYNE REYNOLDS, RICHARD WHITTERS, DAVE KENDALL, CHIPPY

VITHIANS

The humans who fight the good fight are tough, desperate, and inventive. They call themselves "Vithians" after the kingdom of the living that they still attempt to sustain. They employ skill in both battle and magic to protect their lives and their precious vis. Vithian mages set up detection spells and elemental runes to guard their borders from roving necromancers and vampires, and warriors learn battle techniques to defeat the undead. Vithian humans eat whatever they can—mushrooms, rats, scrubby weeds and grasses, even kathari—but don't have much hope for survival. Without some sort of change to the world, humanity will soon become extinct on Grixis.

SKELETONS

Anywhere on Grixis, you can find the animated skeletons of the dead. The skeleton is the common foot soldier of the necromancer's army and personal retinue, but unbound skeletons can also be found. When necromancers die or finally lose their grip on sanity, their skeleton minions are freed from service and roam Grixis, motivated only by an intrinsic hatred for life. Most skeletons you'll encounter are human in origin, the puppeteered remains of ancient Vithians or their present-day descendants. Given a long enough stay on Grixis, you may encounter skeletons that were once other species, such as rats, bats, wolves, viashino, ogres, minotaurs, and rarely, more massive creatures such as baloths, hellions, and dragons. Large, durable skeletons are prized on Grixis, as most skeletons on the plane do not self-reassemble, but rather continue to sustain damage until they are unable to move, rejoining the heaps of scrap corpses that litter the plane.

ZOLTAN BOROS & GABOR SZIKSZAI, COLE EASTBURN

ZOMBIES

A zombie is the reanimated corpse of the preserved dead or recently deceased. Like skeletons, zombies can be made from any dead animal, and are often not humanoid. Zombies retain most of their flesh and structural organs after death, and as a result, often possess greater strength, resilience, and magical aptitude than the fleshless skeletons.

Zombies of Grixis sometimes have a particular tangy scent mixed in with the smell of death and rot. Some necromancers spray concoctions of pickling agents on their living prey before killing them, which allows the zombie's flesh to last much longer than it would otherwise. The smell of pickled flesh should be regarded as a warning— a necromancer's zombie minion is much more dangerous than the free-roaming undead.

Like any undead, zombies are consumed with evil and should be utterly destroyed. Merely slaying a being on Grixis only returns it to the pool of raw materials.

Fleshdolls and Fleshbags

A fleshbag is the flesh of several corpses and/or zombies, sewn together into an amorphous, hollow vessel and filled with some animating element such as banewasps or worms. Fleshbags are usually about the size of a dog or small child, have a few bruised limbs or pseudopods for locomotion, and have little in the way of sensory organs. They tear easily and are not meant for long-term survival, but can be used in a manner similar to blood pets—that is, as living vessels for vis, to be harvested when needed. Occasionally a necromancer will animate a fleshbag using a humanoid ghost, the result of which is called a fleshdoll. Fleshdolls can be enormous, as tall as ogres or even giants, and bloated with spectral energy.

DREG REAVERS

When a necromancer needs a heavy armor unit, he calls on the dreg reavers. These massive, bestial juggernauts have the strength of elephants, the resilience of siege machines, and the damage-dealing capacity of a herd of baloths. Dreg reavers appear in a variety of shapes, all strong and horrible. They can be saddled with war platforms and used as siege engines, or simply set free to wreak massive destruction on a populated area. Some necromancers lash razor wire around the tusks, horns, claws, and tails of dreg reavers, or attach barbed lances to their flanks to augment their pain-inflicting abilities.

INCURABLES

Soon after Alara fractured, a race of ogres in the mountains of Grixis became afflicted with a curse that twisted their anatomies and minds. Their shaman-queen undertook a desperate ritual to dislodge the curse from her people, but instead her magic mutated the curse and strengthened its grasp on them all. Generations of bizarre mutations later, the affliction left these "incurables" monstrous and homicidally insane.

The incurables' curse is potent magic, and may hold the key to more than one race's unfortunate disease. Students of healing and pathomancy are encouraged to travel to Grixis to study the ogres' fate. Their misfortune could reveal answers about the nature of plague and curse magic itself.

BANEWASPS

Banewasps are omnivorous insects that nest in reeflike hives that tower over Grixis's sea. Banewasps prefer decaying flesh to other food and will swarm in great numbers in search of freshly dead corpses. Sometimes banewasp larvae feed on the flesh of still motile creatures, which can cause zombies, or even slightly decrepit humans, to become distended and distorted. Banewasps are poor sources of vis, but can be used by necromancers to animate fleshdolls.

KATHARI

This race of scavenger aven resembles humanoid vultures: a black-winged creature with a bald vulture's head, but humanoid arms and legs. They circle the skies of Grixis, searching for sites of mass death in order to feed on the grisly remains before necromancers get their hands on them. Most kathari are greedy, screeching cowards, but are tolerated among necromancers and lich lords because of the belief that they purge bad luck from the dead.

Kathari practice a religion called Skive, founded on a fervent belief in a higher afterlife. Their scavenging habits go hand-in-hand with their religion, as they believe that cleansing the flesh from the bones of the dead is the only proper form of respect for the deceased, and the only way a soul will be free to enter the afterlife. Kathari nest in aeries in the mountains of Grixis, perched high to avoid marauding undead. They are organized by role into:

Scourers

Nimble warriors who scavenge meat from corpses.

Mediums

Clerics who administer religious rites and speak with the spirits of the dead.

Nestwards

Kathari who maintain and defend aeries.

Caulbreakers

Kathari who tend to the young.

Outcriers

Mystical shamans with black, pupiless eyes who are feared by other kathari. Outcriers are said to boil with the sins of the criminal dead, and can lash out with blasts of dark magic when threatened.

VAMPIRES

Most vampires on Grixis are not the elegant aristocrats that they are on some planes. Here they have very little actual blood to feed upon, so many are reduced to sustaining themselves on the squeezings from corpses and other undead. Their appearance is skeletal,

wretched, and starving. Many have lost the ability to fly, but they can still be fierce, desperate opponents.

Well-fed vampires, on the other hand, flush with the power of vis, soar the storm-choked skies, attracting swarms of bats and other minions. Blood-sated vampires have an almost irresistible aura of power, the attraction of which can be difficult to ignore—even for a planeswalker—so keep your distance.

As life dwindles on Grixis, so does the prospect of survival for its vampiric predators. A conclave of vampires meets at Unx during the darkest nights, to discuss what options they might still have.

DEVILS

No creature gets as much glee from the painful life on Grixis as devils. These smirking, short, red-skinned sadists love to prick and jab at the living, usually to make their last hours as pain-filled as possible. Some devils are employed as torturers by demons, others as cruel slave-drivers for gangs of vitals or packs of undead hounds. Devils are not particularly smart, but are agile and sly. Though their taunts can be maddening, it's best not to attack them—they may be doing the bidding of a much more powerful demonic master. Instead, distract them. The promise of a defenseless victim can sway the mind of even the shrewdest of devils.

DEMONS

Demons are the embodiment of evil. Unnaturally strong, cruelly intelligent, possessed of natural spellcasting abilities, and ageless, they command dark reverence wherever they roam. Demons feed on vis and can extract it directly from a nearby vital host at will, but love causing mortals to surrender their souls voluntarily. Demons can grant an almost unlimited array of powers to mortals in exchange, and cunningly disguise the cost.

Avoidance of demons is strongly recommended, but if you do encounter one and lack the power to destroy it immediately, the best strategy is to become and remain useful to it. One traveler to Grixis survived a demonic encounter by playing the amusing pawn. Another survived by agreeing to become an assassin for the demon, but while she escaped, it is unclear whether her soul remained intact.

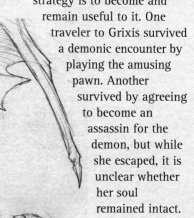

THE DAMNED

Living beings whose soul—and most of their vis—has been surrendered to a demon are known on Grixis as "the Damned." They can be ogres, kathari, or any type of living creature with a soul, but are usually human. The damned have an ashen, gaunt appearance and greatly diminished mental function, but are physiologically alive. As such they can pass for normal humans for a short time, but are completely controlled by their demon masters—making them dangerous spies. Hermitages of the living test for the Damned with rigorous questioning and magical detection.

LICH LORDS

Liches are undead archmages who retain their considerable magical power. They are among the most unnatural beings on Grixis (and that's saying something), and are in constant danger of decaying away. They require a near-constant influx of mana and vis to stay alive, and often position their strongholds on top of rich mana sources.

The undead don't breathe, so they can survive underwater as long as their bodies don't corrode. Under the sea near Kederekt lurks the lich Leogin, the undead form of an archmage who drowned before Vithia fell. Leogin commands huge, putrefied sea beasts capable of devouring whole ships. Death pervades this plane, but personalities persist nevertheless. As of this printing, the following are important figures on Grixis.

Eliza of the Keep

Young, shrewd, and hauntingly beautiful, Eliza is a human necromancer who has schemed and bullied her way to a position of power, all while keeping hold of her precious mortal life. Eliza commands a legion of undead from her stronghold at Ilson Gate. Eliza routinely requires the vis of the living to retain her vitality, so her legions are constantly scouting for villages and raiding ogre lairs.

Thraximundar

No battlefield is safe from Thraximundar, a brutal undead warrior who slays to live. He is fully seven feet tall and rippling with dead muscle, clad in dreadful spiked armor and wielding a greatsword. Astride his massive dreg reaver mount like some dark parody of a knight, Thraximundar—whose name means "he who paints the earth red"—is drawn to the sounds and emotions of mass violence. He never takes sides—he slays anyone, taking grim pleasure in the pure act of war itself.

Malfegor

Said to be born from an unthinkable union, Malfegor is a demonic dragon—a dragon with a demonic soul. With scales like shiny black plates, a powerful, eight-limbed body, and enormous, batlike wings, Malfegor is the essence of both power and fury. However, though he is loath to take orders, it is said that Malfegor answers to one other. Malfegor's master may lurk somewhere on Grixis, or outside the plane entirely.

JUND

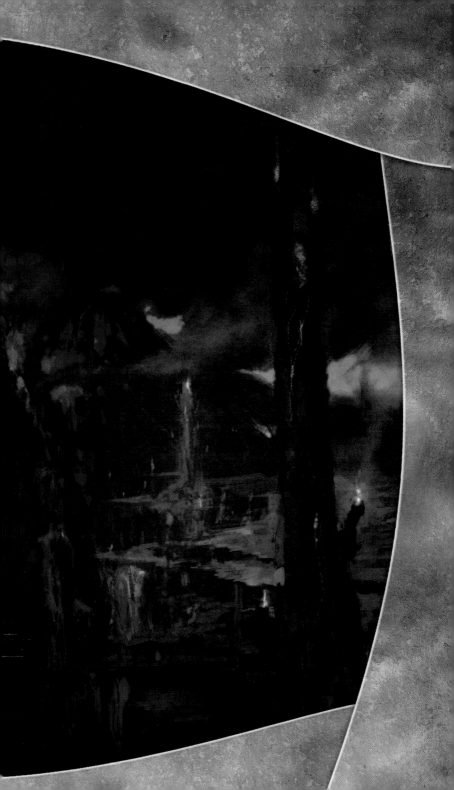

THE PLANE OF JUND

In Jund, everything wants to kill you. With a landscape of rocky volcanoes, primal jungles, and treacherous tar pits, Jund is a savage world teeming with poisonous plants and dominated by reptilian life. While Jund is home to three main humanoid races—humans, crocodilian viashino, and lowly goblins—it's the dragons who are the undisputed tyrants of this plane. Lords of the sky, dragons soar across the blood-red horizon looking for anything foolish enough to venture into the open.

Sitting comfortably at the top of the food chain, dragons ruthlessly possess the high ground and consider other beings that venture there to be their rightful prey. They establish territory by challenging and defeating other dragons and eating their rivals. Though intelligent dragons exist elsewhere, the dragons of Jund are about slaughter, not sentience.

Viashino

Viashino are brutish predators, fairly unintelligent and with minimal society. They form groups called "thrashes" that live and hunt in well-defined territories in the swampy lowland jungles. Expert ambushers, viashino warriors are able to wait patiently for days then move with alarming speed to make the kill.

Humans

Humans divide into tribal groups out of necessity rather than a sense of communal bonding—a large group of warriors hunting together has better odds of a kill than a warrior hunting alone. Dozens of different human tribes occupy territory mostly on the cliffs overlooking the valleys and canyons. Both men and women are warriors, shamans, and chieftains—the harsh laws of survival ultimately determine rank and influence.

Goblins

Goblins of Jund are terribly debased beings that have been at the bottom of the pecking order for so long that they now find glory in being eaten by dragons. Despite their perverse pride in being "divine food," they believe in making a good show of things, so they still try their best to survive. Goblins are not dragons' favored prey—they're scrawny little nuggets—but they are useful to stave off hunger as a dragon searches for an actual meal.

HIGH GROUND, LOW GROUND

Because of the undisputed supremacy of dragons, a geographical hierarchy has emerged among humanoids. As the weakest race, goblins occupy the highest ground, such as inhospitable mountainsides and barren plateaus, which makes them easy prey for cruising dragons.

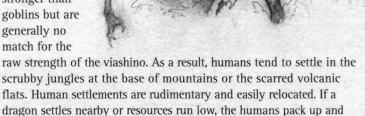

Humans are stronger than goblins but are generally no match for the raw strength of the viashino. As a result, humans tend to settle in the scrubby jungles at the base of mountains or the scarred volcanic flats. Human settlements are rudimentary and easily relocated. If a dragon settles nearby or resources run low, the humans pack up and move to a more hospitable location.

Jund's surface is covered with deep gashes that resemble claw marks. The deepest of these, the Rip, plunges nearly two miles from the scarred hilltops to its swampy, jungle-filled depths. The viashino control these canyons with brute strength and tactical cunning. On the low ground under the forest canopy, they are generally safe from dragon predation, and guard their coveted territory with fang and claw.

SANGRITE

Sangrite forms as reddish cylindrical spikes in volcanoes or deep caverns. These distinctive formations of crystallized energy are one of the great mysteries of Jund and have attracted many travelers who hope to harness their power.

No one knows how sangrite is created, but some believe that when a creature dies on Jund, its life-force disperses into the air and settles in crystals that already exist in volcanoes and caves. Others point to the thick concentrations in dragons' lairs as evidence that sangrite is a crystallized form of dragon's breath that contains the life-force of its prey.

The potential power of sangrite is undisputed. Infused with life essence, crushed sangrite is an incredibly potent form of energy. Dragons sometimes consume entire crystals, which grant them intense, but short-lived, strength and power.

CICATRICE

This is a region of especially rugged land, knuckled and twisted between two great rift valleys. Called scar-lands by the tribes that live in this extreme terrain, the Cicatrice is home to one of the most powerful of Jund's dragons, a red-scaled, tattered-winged monstrosity whose shadow blots out the sun and casts her quarry into darkness. She has several nests here but keeps her main hoard in an obsidian basin ringed with talonlike spikes.

THE BLOODHALL

This consecrated cavern is in the scar-lands above the rift valleys. The cave is sacred to humans, but in territory unclaimed by any tribe. A narrow chasm carved by a long-defunct geyser penetrates the rock at a steep angle. At the bottom of the chasm is the Bloodhall, a circular room with red sangrite coating the walls with a glassy sheen. It is here that humans gather for the Life Hunt, a sacred ritual where a select group of warriors kill a dragon—or fight it until none of them are left alive.

WORLDHEART CHALICE

There are rumors of a volcanic cavern filled with shards of sangrite larger than a dragon, as well as the most unique formation of all: a colossal crimson helix that is the backbone of the mountain itself. It is said that Worldheart sangrite pulses with the spirits of creatures far more powerful than dragons—the ancient ones that reigned before Alara split. There is a legend that three planeswalkers made a wager to see who could find a piece of the crimson sangrite. Only one man returned from Jund with the coveted crystal, but he went insane. The other two dueled over the spoils, until one lay dying on the ground. The other disappeared with his prize and was never heard from again.

DRAGONS OF JUND

While dragons are fiercely protective of their hunting grounds and nests, they can roam far from their lairs, and the skies are governed by a different set of rules. In the air, dragons will sometimes fly together, almost playfully. They display feats of acrobatic daring and companionship that would be unthinkable closer to the ground, where dragons will kill a rival over a measly goblin stolen from their territory.

Dragons have varied hunting techniques based on the type of prey. When attacking a large creature, dragons swoop from the sky and inflict a single disabling bite. The dragon then circles high above until the creature bleeds out. When the prey is too weak to fight back, the dragon eats it at its leisure.

Currents of black volcanic haze drift across Jund's skies, and these clouds provide cover for even the largest dragons, who can glide across open ground unseen and destroy an entire settlement. Because most adult dragons can satisfy their hunger on humans and other beasts, dragons that hunt viashino do so for sport rather than food. Dragons can occasionally be seen cruising directly above the "rivers" of forest in the canyons, diving between the trees with powerful grace to pluck an unsuspecting viashino from the ground.

THE CYCLE OF LIFE

Dragons don't reproduce often. A female dragon might lay eggs only once every twenty years. Eggs are hidden in a cleft or a fumarole in the side of a volcano within their mother's territory to keep them warm for the year they need to hatch. The parent tolerates the young dragon in her territory for a while, but once they have grown to the size of horses, she treats them as rivals and might even kill them if they don't leave.

Finding new territory is difficult, so the young dragon must either settle for inferior land or try to wrest a holding from another. During this phase of its life, it is an eating machine. Such young dragons are the greatest threats to creatures in the valleys because they can't afford to be picky about where they hunt and will slaughter anything they can.

THE SHRIEK OF FLAME

Dragons don't go peacefully into death. When an ancient has become too feeble to defend its territory, it goes out with a bang. In a ritual known as the Shriek of Flame, a dragon finds an unstable volcano, flies high above the crater, then plunges in a shrieking death-dive straight into the magma. A fiery cataclysm erupts on impact, and many lowland groups believe all volcanic eruptions are caused by the death of a dragon.

VIASHINO

While the jungles offer some protection from dragons, they have their own set of dangers. Tar elementals, oozes, and lizards of all sizes share the swampy floor with the viashino, and many plants have moved beyond mere toxicity and have developed attack strategies of their own.

Viashino males generally lead the thrashes: they are heavy-set, muscular creatures that resemble humanoid alligators. The whole group is nomadic, though, so the females also hunt and fight—and when they're protecting clutches of eggs, they can overpower males larger than themselves.

WEAPONS OF WAR

Viashino weapons are simple, usually clubs studded with chips of obsidian or teeth.

Kikkach

The paddle-shaped club lined with the teeth of crocodiles or predatory dinosaurs is called a *kikkach*, which means "rasping tongue"—like that of a great cat.

Sshak

A *sshak* is a crude axe carved from a large animal's bone, with chips of obsidian along the cutting edge. The name is an onomatopoeic name for the sound of its strike.

Challik

Some viashino use a type of grappling hook that launches jagged, heavy stones attached to cords that let them draw in entangled prey. The word *challik*, translates as "toad's tongue."

A viashino hunter is also prone to wade into the fight with its own impressive natural weaponry. Its powerful bite and clawed limbs can inflict horrendous damage.

Sneak Attack

Viashino are masters of the ambush, lying in wait for beasts or human hunting parties. Sometimes a viashino party will raid a human settlement, stealing children or other objects of value to lure the humans onto the canyon floor. The viashino conceal themselves in the murky channels that wind across the jungle floor, sometimes for days, waiting for the warriors to pass. This tactic works surprisingly well: slay the humans, keep the spoils, and have several days worth of fresh meat for the entire thrash.

Viashino Thrashes

Viashino live together in hunting bands called thrashes. Brute strength determines who leads the thrash, and once established, the leader makes all decisions for the viashino in his band. The personality of the leader affects how a thrash hunts and where it lives. When a leader is killed, a thrash often will change its name and move to a new hunting ground.

Palehide Thrash

This thrash prides itself on slaying humans, which they call "palehides." They're aggressive and largely nomadic, following what weaker human tribes they can find. Their leader is an old, brittle-scaled viashino named Igh who claims to have personally slain three hundred humans in his lifetime.

Pitch Thrash

This thrash rules a vast network of low-lying tar pits known as the Seethe. Leadership changes often; the black mana of the Seethe causes these viashino to be more treacherous and merciless than other thrashes. The thrash specializes in running its prey into the pits and trapping them in the quagmire.

Manytooth Thrash

This thrash prides itself on the might and viciousness of its warriors. They seek out other thrashes against which to test themselves, and over time have earned a very large territory for themselves. The Manytooth have a coming-of-age ritual that involves young viashino fighting to the death for the right to become full-fledged warriors of the thrash.

HUMANS

For humans, relationships are fleeting, and the death rate
extremely high. A person over thirty is considered old and anyone
who makes it to fifty is ancient. Humans sometimes have features
that mimic reptiles, such as forked tongues or pseudo-scales
covering parts of their skin. Combat is the one constant in every
human's life.

The tukatongue tree is the primary food staple for humans, and a
tribe without access to a tukatongue struggles for survival.
Growing on high plateaus, the tree's supple wood and tough bark
helps it survive fierce winds and a marauding dragon's fiery breath.
The tree's roots can be ground into a sticky paste for an unappealing,
but reliable, food source. Many stone weapons are wrapped in the
spiky bark to add gash to smash. Humans live in temporary shelters
made from tuka frames and covered in lizard skin—a viashino hide
is a sign of social status. From a distance these round huts look like
the backs of giant turtles.

The Dark Climb

When they reach the age of ten, children are sent on a quest known as the Dark Climb. Alone and unarmed, a child is sent into the mountains in search of a shard of volcanic glass. This task is extremely hazardous. Not only are the fiery mountains dangerous in themselves, but they are the favored roosts of young dragons. By this age, most children have already faced viashino and dragon attacks, and many are quite resourceful as they make their way into the volcanic peaks.

Those who return home with a shard are given an obsidian weapon, which is crafted from their hard-earned volcanic glass and annealed with shamanic magic. Legends are born from these quests. Breot the Slayer survived forty days alone in the mountain. His tribe assumed he was dead and moved far down the Rift Valley. But Breot tracked them down, hauling the carcass of a dead gharlizard on his back, with his obsidian shard still lodged in its throat.

Shamanic Circle

Children with natural ability are raised within the shamans' enclosure, where they learn the ways of the spirits until their tenth birthday. But unlike the Dark Climb, which tests future warriors, the rite known as the Shamanic Circle tests the child's magical strength.

The child is brought before the full Shamanic Circle and given the Dreamfire Draught, a potent drug—and slow-acting poison—that causes the child to become a magnet for elemental entities. The circle collectively summons a wild elemental into the circle, and the child must bargain with the elemental for a boon to stop the poison. Success means survival and entry into the circle as an adept. Shamans are highly respected, ranking even higher than a tribe's warrior chieftain. In battle, the shamans summon elementals to fight for their people.

Battle-Token Braids

Honor and social status among humans are defined by prowess in combat and warfare. Warriors who return with a trophy of the hunt earn a mark of achievement—a twisted braid bound with a bit of skin or tendon from a fallen enemy. Shamans take this further and tie bones, tusks, fur, and other such trophies into their hair. The more braids, the higher their social rank. However, only significant kills are so marked—a simple food-gathering hunt or repelling a motley thrash of viashino is not enough to earn a braid. Only a few heroes wear more than five braids; a dozen is the stuff of legend.

LIFE HUNT

This greatest of all human rituals begins with a vision of a dragon falling out of the sky. Every eight years, a different shaman is mysteriously gifted with this sight, and he or she becomes the Vision Shaman. The Vision Shaman summons the most decorated hunters of all the tribes to a gather in the Bloodhall. Together these warriors must hunt and kill a dragon. All are expected to fight to the death, and it is a great dishonor to desert the hunt while any warriors are still alive.

More often than not, the dragon is victorious, and the once proud warriors become carrion for starving goblins. Some of the tribes have begun to refuse the summons of the Vision Shaman. Why sacrifice their strongest warriors to a futile cause when there is enough threat from dragons without seeking one in its nest?

HIGHCLAN TOL HERA

This human tribe, led by the impetuous Javid Hera, believes that humans should not skulk in the low ground but take possession of the heights. To them, the Life Hunt should not be a rare ceremony but an ongoing war against the dragons until one or the other side is exterminated. Unlike other tribes, these humans see no evil in consuming the life energy stored in sangrite crystals to increase their own power. Their numbers are small, however, in large part due to their bold forays into the high ground, but every member of the tribe is a fearsome combatant as a result.

THE WARRIOR KRESH

The Tol Hera tribe has the greatest of the human champions, Kresh. He is almost forty years old and wears twenty-two braids—more than any other alive. He has survived three Life Hunts. The identity of his parents is unknown; he was rescued from a burning village by Tol Hera warriors as an infant. His word carries great authority when tribal councils are called and on the Life Hunts themselves. He doesn't want the headaches of leadership, living for the hunt beyond all things, so he has never challenged the chief of his tribe.

VANCE KOVACS, RAYMOND SWANLAND

GOBLINS

Most goblins live in cairnlike "shelter stones" that are heaped up to keep off the worst predator attacks. Scavengers who pick the bones of old kills, goblins also eat insects and worms, and gather the roots and tough fruit of the sparse vegetation that grows on mountainsides and plateaus.

Most goblins are spindly in build, but stronger than they appear and very fast. They can wriggle into spaces a snake would have second thoughts about. The word for squirming into a tight crack—a goblin's preferred escape tactic—is the somewhat poetic phrase *plikintok agat,* or "wearing a garment of rock."

They wield primitive weapons made of their ancestors' bones, especially femurs and ribs, and a leader carries a mace crafted from the skull of his or her predecessor.

Desperation Raids

Starving groups of goblins will sometimes organize raids on the more verdant lands below them. These raids are usually a disaster, however. Raiders are picked off one-by-one by predators, carnivorous plants, or their own incompetence—or the entire party is devoured by a fire elemental or some other monstrosity. The goal of such raids is for at least one goblin to return with food for at least two. The unspoken truth about these raids is that they're a form of population control.

NAYA

The Plane of Naya

Welcome to Naya, where the jungle is king. Here natural wonders of astounding beauty are veiled by lush forests or secreted between steep mountains. Growth is accelerated by the warm, wet climate, and some of Naya's animals have reached an awesome scale. Known as gargantuans, these behemoth creatures are revered as gods.

Leonin, elves, and humans are the most common races in Naya—there are rumors of minotaurs in the caves in the mountains, but that could simply be campfire tales. Archeological records show that the leonins were once the undisputed masters of this plane. But internal strife shattered their empire and now the leonins are scattered and disorganized. Today, in the race for dominance, the elves are winning.

Nacatl

The mountains are home to the Nacatl leonin. Like lions, the males have manes. But the coloration of their coats ranges from mottled-jaguar to silver-gray to totally black. Scattered across the mountains are Nacatl ruins, shattered and half-covered in vines and flowers. With the fall of the Empire of the Clouds, there was a division in the race. Cloud Nacatl maintain an opulent lifestyle in the remaining mountaintop fortresses while the Wild Nacatl have returned to a feral existence.

HUMANS

Impulsive and unbound, the humans that dwell on the jungle floor have invented ingenious ways to survive in the most hostile environment in Naya. Rainfall is the lifeblood of the jungle, and vegetation is in a constant race, always clawing upward in the competition for sunshine. When a tree falls in the jungle, a massive hole is punctured in the canopy. Thousands of seeds are waiting for the chance to grow and fill the space, but the humans bring in the plowbeasts to beat back the natural world. Often they will have a rudimentary structure built within a few days, with a herd of pip fawns to eat the green shoots before they can reclaim the precious open space.

CYLIAN ELVES

Nomadic canopy dwellers, the elves have a spiritual connection to the gargantuans. The elves live in brightly colored silk tents and congregate around dewcups, pools of water that gather in the canopy's giant ferns. Elves are territorial, but in a convoluted sense, with shifting allegiances and complicated boundaries. There's an elven saying about leaving their handprint in the air. It's the idea that by living somewhere for a time, they then claim a fleeting ownership over that area of the canopy.

119

Cloud Jungles

In the mountains, there is sunshine in the morning followed by rainstorms in the afternoon, and mist that rolls in at dusk. When the sun is shining, the jade-green leaves and colorful cascades of flowers stand out in startling contrast against the golden sky.

But in the evenings, the air is cooler and the fog settles on the jungle like a heavy hand. It is unusually quiet under the trees when the mist engulfs the mountains. Called Whitecover, this fog is so thick it's almost tangible. Even the non-superstitious Nacatl believe certain creatures emerge from their hiding places during Whitecover—creatures that are never seen by the light of day.

There are volcanoes in the mountains—erupting perhaps once a decade—as well as an extensive and largely unexplored system of caves. Most gargantuans live in the lowlands, but a few inhabit the caves and mountaintops.

CANOPY AND FLOOR

In the lowlands, trees grow to incredible heights as they compete for space and sunlight. The canopy is laced together by massive lianas—thick, woody vines that connect the trees and can grow up to five feet in diameter. Animals, humans, and elves use these lianas as highways to travel across the jungle. On Naya, color means danger: purple flesh-eating flowers, red blood-sucking snakes, and fuchsia fungus vines are some of the species that flaunt their deadliness.

Whereas the elves inhabit the canopy, humans live on the jungle floor, which is a darker, humid, and more treacherous place than the canopy. Most species that inhabit the lowest level of Naya are forced to survive from what falls from above: specks of light, dead leaves, and over-ripe fruit. Amid the massive buttress roots are termites, fungi, and oversized logger-ants who hunt by scent and can easily take down an unsuspecting human or elf.

Gargantuans

Gargantuans dominate life on Naya. Most are mammalian carnivores that wander where they please and crush a human village or gulp down a tribe of elves without warning. During a rampage, they can alter the course of a river or shave off a large section of a mountain. Some of them are so big that they create their own climate. The smaller races seek ways to control, or at least understand, these behemoths that share Naya with them. The elves believe the gargantuans to be manifestations of the will of Progenitus, the so-called Soul of the World and the life spirit of Naya.

Godtrackers

The best warriors of the elves, they track the movement of the gargantuans, ignoring all territorial boundaries. They tend to stir up skirmishes wherever they go. Godtrackers report the activities of the gargantuans to the Anima, the elves' high priest.

Epicists

Based on the information of the Godtrackers, these elves write epic poetry that records the behavior and battles of the gargantuans. This information helps the Anima and druids better cull the signs and therefore better understand Progenitus, Soul of the World.

The elves see the humans as spiritual infants and are willing to help keep them from getting squished by the gargantuans, but they're not so sharing with the Nacatl. They would prefer the Nacatl stay in the mountains and stop wandering in the lowlands.

THE ELVES OF NAYA

The humans call them Canopy Elves. The Nacatl call them Vinewalkers. But they call themselves Cylian elves after the first high priest, Cylia the Witness, who was present at the Breaking of the World.

The high priest of the elves, called the Anima, is chosen from a line of female druids who have proven that they have a connection with the gargantuans. Whether the creatures are a force for destruction or creation, the elves believe all of the gargantuans' actions must be interpreted and considered in future actions.

The Sacellum is the spiritual home of the elves. The anima and her attendants and guardians reside in this living cathedral crafted by druids who shape roots into architecture. With walls of roots, vines, and leaves, the Sacellum is a cavernous room with holes cut in the canopy and draped with colored silks, letting colored light filter into the space. Flowers grow out of the walls, and a host of small jungle animals—lemurs, small cats, tiny fawnlike creatures—make this place their home.

PROGENITUS, SOUL OF THE WORLD

"The elves believe that Progenitus sleeps in the Valley of the Ancients, his body covered by a millennia of growth."

And the world shattered. While the elves cowered in terror at the cataclysm, young Cylia climbed to the top of the mountain armed with a vial of poison and a dagger crafted from a thorn. On the summit she saw the face of Progenitus, the five-headed Soul of the World.

Progenitus had grown tired of creation and unleashed five storms to consume it: Wildfire, Earthquake, Windstorm, Flood, and Void. Cylia begged Progenitus not to scour life from the world. Furious at her impudence, Progenitus blinded the girl and turned to watch the cleansing of creation. With blood from her mutilated eyes dripping into the vial, Cylia dipped the dagger into the poison and closed her senses to the destruction. In her stillness she could hear each note of creation's death song. She could feel the interconnected threads of all life, from the terror of the fawn cowering in the forest to the heartbeat of the hawk soaring helplessly in the tempestuous sky.

Cylia shifted through the invisible strands until she found the one mystical connection to Progenitus, and she flung her poisoned dagger straight into its ethereal heart. With that one blow, Progenitus's nature was revealed to be a five-headed hydra.

THE NOMADIC LIFESTYLE

Except for the Anima and her court, the elves move around the jungle in loosely organized groups based more around friendship than bloodline. All swear allegiance to the Anima, and make frequent pilgrimages to the Sacellum for advice on how to keep Progenitus from killing them.

The elves are constantly on the move. They use up all available resources then find a new home. Wanat trees are the major year-round food source. Their nuts are high in protein and their flowers make an energy-enhancing drink. Elves don't keep much property, but what they do have is ornamental with fine details and embroidery.

Sunsail Tents

The elves live in brightly colored silk tents that are set in sharp angles in the trees. Elves congregate around dewcups, which are oasis-like gathering places in the canopy. With abundant resources, it's not difficult for elves to find enough to eat, so a lot of time is spent in social interactions. If one group runs into another, everyone sits inside the silk tents, has a glass of lotus-drink, and talks for a long time. At the end of such a meeting, it's customary to make a verbal exchange of all their worldly possessions, immediately exchange them back, and watch to make sure that the other group moves an acceptable distance away.

The Valley of the Ancients

Valley Wards are the elves who watch the Valley of the Ancients and monitor Progenitus at rest under centuries of jungle growth. The elves constantly monitor his sleep. There are three steam vents that release air at regular intervals—the slow, even breath of Progenitus at rest.

Chirin of the Valley is an older elf who has been a Valley Ward for almost thirty years and knows the landscape of the Valley of the Ancients better than anyone. Fifteen years ago he witnessed the Second Stirring when Progenitus began to awaken, tearing the vegetation from its roots and ripping off huge sections of nearby mountains. The elves believe that only the close connection of the Anima and quick sacrifices kept Progenitus under the ground.

The Gear of a Valley Ward

Most of the wards are musicians of some kind, and the lilting sounds of a flute can often be heard in the Valley of the Ancients. Here are two kinds of glass lanterns, each containing a colorful viscous liquid that rises as it heats. The staff is handy for hooking jungle animals that get too familiar with a ward's food supply. And the mask is a token of good fortune—may Progenitus be sated through his gargantuans!

RICHARD WHITTERS, KEV WALKER

THE NACATL

High in the mountains, the leonin built a sophisticated empire, and for centuries they were the undisputed rulers of Naya. In its heyday, the Empire of the Clouds had an extensive system of roads, including tunnels, towers, and bridges—all constructed out of rocks and timbers so finely cut that mortar was unnecessary. Aqueducts brought water to their mountain cities, and the Nacatl carved mountainsides into terraced farmland. Today, the Nacatl civilization has fallen into ruins.

The Nacatl social unit is the pride. Among the Cloud Nacatl, prides are longstanding and complex familial structures with their own great histories and bloodlines. The Wild Nacatl, however, have prides that are looser and more changeable. Each pride has a leader—an "alpha male"—though individuals within the pride generally have the freedom to do as they wish. Leadership and status are determined through ferocity and survival rather than blood ties.

The Cloud Empire

During the years of the empire, the Nacatl didn't have a spiritual culture. In their worldview, the gargantuans that roam Naya were simply the product of the climate and abundant resources, not manifestations of Progenitus. The Nacatl embraced a code of ethics called the Coil in which each was free to pursue happiness however they wanted as long as they didn't hurt another Nacatl.

The Nacatl chiseled the details of the Coil in their pseudo-written language on the Binding Wall, a massive white granite slab outside of Antali, the capital of the Empire of the Clouds. By the time the empire fell, the Coil had become so complicated and convoluted that most Nacatl couldn't follow it even if they wanted to. The Coil was enforced at first by societal pressure and later by the Pride of Judges, an elite group of Nacatl who carried a coil of rope, which looked disturbingly like a noose, and would loop it over an offender's door.

THE CLAWS OF MARISI

As the Nacatl Empire expanded, it faced internal pressures as some Nacatl prospered under the Coil and the division of wealth became uneven. Some argued that the Nacatl had abandoned their true feline nature, which was warlike and nomadic. Under the empire, the Nacatl had become soft and corrupted.

For decades this low-level discontent rotted the civilization from the inside, with more and more Nacatl turning away from the Coil. The situation came to a head when a young Nacatl named Marisi formed an anti-civilization group known as the Claws of Marisi. After years of simmering discontent, Marisi rallied a huge uprising against the Empire of the Clouds. Many cities were sacked and burned.

During the destruction of Antali, the wall was defaced and in some parts smashed. For the members of the Claw, it was a symbolic breaking of the strictures of society that kept them down and subjugated their warrior nature.

ZOLTAN BOROS & GABOR SZIKSZAI, WAYNE REYNOLDS

Qasal: The Last Stronghold

Qasal is the last remaining stronghold of the Cloud Nacatl. Though highly fortified, there's little hope that its residents are going to be able to maintain their opulent lifestyle for much longer. With the unique coloring of an ocelot, Timus the Orange rules the mountaintop fortress as if he were king. Only his keen intelligence and strategic nature keeps the city functioning.

While stonework is used in the construction of roads and large buildings, the Nacatl prefer to live in drays: small, stone-hewn dens built around tree trunks and in cliff faces. The Nacatl like baskets and reed weaving, and decorate their drays with remnants of their warrior past, like old shields, weapons, and exquisite tusk carvings. Celebration and wealth are highly prized among the Nacatl.

EMERGENCE OF THE WILD NACATL

Most Nacatl have returned to wandering the cloud jungles and grow more feral with each generation. Many have returned to a mainly nocturnal existence, sleeping in low branches during the day and doing most of their hunting in the early evening. Starstalkers are the most skilled hunters of the Wild Nacatl, and are highly respected for their physical prowess.

Many nomadic tribes camp in the ruins of their former civilization. Because of fewer resources in the high jungles, the Nacatl have begun wandering into the lower elevations, where they fight both elves and humans over territory.

THE HUMANS OF NAYA

Humans live on the jungle floor, the harshest environment in Naya. But in the dim world under the canopy, among the massive buttress roots of the towering trees, the humans are intent on making the most of their existence. For the humans, it's all about pleasure—the pleasure of the hunt, the pleasure of the body, the pleasure of celebration, and the pleasure of competition.

Drumhunting

Humans hunt in packs and communicate by drumming and knocking on buttress roots in a practice called drumhunting. Roots have distinct sounds, so everyone can identify where a particular group is located and coordinate hunting maneuvers.

Bloodthorn Trees

The short, bushy bloodthorn trees have long, poisonous thorns with a hook at the end. If they remain in the skin too long they're fatal. But humans have developed an immunity and sometimes build their settlements inside bloodthorn groves. The middle of the thicket is hollowed out, leaving a ring of bloodthorn trees as a barrier against predators.

Scarlet Wasp

These particularly deadly wasps build huge nests in the trees. One sting can kill a medium-sized animal. As they have with bloodthorn trees, humans have cultivated an immunity to the sting of the scarlet wasp, and often build near their huge nests for protection. In small doses, the wasp toxin can be distilled into an elixir that provides humans with increased strength.

The River Wild

Water is the wild card in human existence. Jungle rivers are dangerously unpredictable. When they flood, as they often do, the river's edge swallows huge sections of the forest, forming landlocked lakes. The unpredictable waterways constantly redesign the jungle tapestry, destroying the open spaces and settlements that humans work so hard to create.

JIM MURRAY, STEVE ARGYLE, WAYNE REYNOLDS, CYRIL VAN DER HAEGEN

THE EXUBERANTS

There is an increasing divide between the humans who live in hollowed buttress roots in the jungle and rely on hunting for food and the humans who are experimenting with agriculture and domesticating animals.

Humans who make their home in the small cities within the jungle are referred to as the Exuberants. They are a hedonistic, vital group adept at living in the moment, providing luxury and relaxation for drumhunters as they move from place to place. They also host competitions and make sacrifices of food and precious objects as the elves instruct.

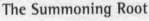

The Summoning Root

The base of the largest tree in the lowlands, which covers several acres and has the loudest and most distinctive sound of all, is called the Summoning Root. When there is an emergency, humans summon all groups to that spot by drumming on the root in a specific rhythm. The emergency summons is so loud that the vibrations can be felt on the streets of Qasal, high in the mountains.

Sunseeders

More humans are building permanent settlements and villages in the few open areas that exist in Naya. Calling themselves Sunseeders, their quest for open sky is developing spiritual proportions. Led by a charismatic man named Hadran, the Sunseeders are undergoing an agrarian revolution and are creating more open spaces for cultivating crops.

In addition to plow beasts, humans keep griffins tethered on long cords near their fields. Part guard animal and part familiar, griffins are often decorated with colorful leather straps and embroidered cloth. Every group of Sunseeders has a herd of pip fawns as well. About the size of a goat, pip fawns are cultivated for meat and milk. Because of the massive amount of grass and plants they eat, the size of pip fawn herds are carefully managed. If a herd is too big, it will attract the gargantuans.

Matca

Humans use open spaces as a place to play games, feel the sun, and engage in any number of pleasurable activities. Matca is the most popular game among humans. It's basically a grappling match, where you wrestle with your opponent until one person is pinned on their back. The hard-core wrestlers wear spiky armor. There are massive arenas and Matca matches draw huge crowds—and even the occasional elf.

THE PLANESWALKERS OF ALARA

As a planeswalker, you know that the people and personalities of a plane are among its greatest treasures. But you must also know that other planeswalkers can be among a plane's greatest threats. For this reason we share with you profiles of the four planeswalkers currently known to reside among Alara's shards, including two who are native to the shards. Some planeswalkers other than these four may have traveled through Alara in recent memory, leaving behind traces in the æther. But if they did, they hid it well. Here we provide detail only about those planeswalkers whose presence has been confirmed.

The following profiles are not intended to be comprehensive assessments of the planeswalkers' abilities nor judgments of their character. Approach other planeswalkers at your own risk. The publishers of A PLANESWALKER'S GUIDE do not guarantee that these planeswalkers currently inhabit the planes listed, do not claim that the list of profiled planeswalkers is exhaustive, and are not liable for personal injury or property damage sustained as a result of the information provided herein.

VOLKAN BAGA

144

ELSPETH TIREL

SPECIES: Human female

PLANE OF ORIGIN: Unknown

PLANE OF CURRENT RESIDENCE: Bant

SPECIALTIES:
Humanoid summoning,
protection of others

Elspeth's past is a bit of a mystery to those around her. She became a squire to a knight of the Bantian nation of Valeron at age seventeen, and was knighted at twenty. But she is not from Valeron, and she evades questions about her childhood. In truth, she was born on another plane, a place of strife and darkness. Her planeswalker spark ignited when she was just thirteen years of age, and after leaving her home plane, she never returned. Elspeth sought a plane she could call home, a place that had what her true home lacked: peace, love, and community. She found them in Bant.

Elspeth's most notable trait as a planeswalker is that she doesn't want to be one anymore; she has no desire to planeswalk. Though she hasn't seen many planes, she believes Bant is a true utopia, the best place in the Multiverse. Her heart's desire is to protect her adopted homeland and its people, and to be among them, as one of them, as well as she can.

ANTHONY FRANCISCO

TEZZERET

SPECIES: Human male
(with etherium enhancements)
PLANE OF ORIGIN: Esper
PLANE OF CURRENT RESIDENCE: Unknown
SPECIALTIES:
Artifice,
mental magic

Tezzeret is intelligent, resourceful, and self-sufficient. He has a deep curiosity and a great hunger for secrets, and is not above using some manipulation to get what he wants. Tezzeret became an initiate of an Esper sect called the Seekers of Carmot not because he believed in their teachings, but because he wanted to see for himself the Codex Etherium, a sacred tome the sect claims to have in its possession.

When he intruded into the sanctum of the Seekers of Carmot, he was caught, and the resulting battle nearly cost him his life. But during the battle Tezzeret's planeswalker spark was ignited, enabling his escape. Even as he reels from the sudden knowledge of other planes adjacent to his own, he worked to discover the real force behind the Seekers of Carmot.

DAARKEN

148

SARKHAN VOL

SPECIES: Human male

PLANE OF ORIGIN: Unknown

PLANE OF CURRENT RESIDENCE: Jund

SPECIALTIES:

Creature magic,

dragon summoning

Sarkhan Vol comes from a plane where territorial warlords vie against each other in unending, brutal war. On this plane, dragons have long since been hunted to extinction for sport and glory. Beforehe became a planeswalker, Vol belonged to a shamanic circle that venerated the dragon as the ultimate predator, the purest expression of the consuming urge of all life.

During a deep shamanic trance, Sarkahn Vol made contact with the spirit of an ancient dragon, and it was during this transcendental moment that his planeswalker spark ignited. On the realization that other planes existed beyond his own, Vol began his quest to understand the draconic spirit, to find a plane where he could look a dragon in the eye.

After many years of searching the planes, he found Jund, a place where dragons reign. He has remained in Jund for nearly two years, trying to find a way to make a spiritual connection with a worthy dragon.

AJANI GOLDMANE

SPECIES: Leonin male
PLANE OF ORIGIN: Naya
PLANE OF CURRENT RESIDENCE: Naya
SPECIALTIES:

Protection of others,

inspiring the souls of others,

justice magic

Ajani Goldmane is a Nacatl leonin and a native of Naya. He has a scar over his left eye and carries a double-bladed axe, his own signature weapon fused with that of his fallen brother. Ajani's brother, the leader of their pride, was killed by an assassin with unknown motives. As Ajani has failed to reassemble the pride or to find any clues about the identity of his brother's killer, he has grown more unstable and has begun to confuse righteous passion with anger, justice with revenge. Furthermore, his own pride may turn against him, blaming him for their leader's death.

As Ajani's planeswalker spark ignited, the reality of planes beyond Naya complicated his situation. The trail of clues about his brother's murder led him away from Naya and into the wider world of Alara—and into a grander plot that he is just beginning to perceive. As Ajani's quest grows in scale, so does his potential as a mage, as he finds power in the violent emotions swirling inside him.

Leaving Alara

From Esper's wind-scoured Cliffs of Ot to Jund's jungle-choked Rip chasm, from the bygone opulence of Naya's Antali ruins to the decaying necropolis at Unx on the plane of Grixis, Alara offers more than any planeswalker could experience in a lifetime, let alone a short planeswalk. This guide can only scratch the surface of the sights and sounds Alara has in store; we hope you'll be inspired now to plan your trip to the shards to encounter even more.

Like any plane in the Multiverse, Alara has a troubled past and an uncertain future. It's the planeswalker's mission to brave the dangers of as many planes as possible and drink deep of the experiences there, to serve as the bridges of sentient contact between worlds, and to invest in one's own soul by enriching it with the countless stories of the Multiverse. Every plane is a moment in time; you, planeswalker, are its only hope of immortality.

DAN SEAGRAVE